A Midsummer Night's Dream

Retold by Robert Swindells

Illustrated by Tomislav Tomic

A & C Black • London

First published 2009 by
A & C Black Publishers Ltd
36 Soho Square, London, W1D 3QY

www.acblack.com

Text copyright © 2009 Robert Swindells
Illustrations copyright © 2009 Tomislav Tomic

The rights of Robert Swindells and Tomislav Tomic to be
identified as author and illustrator of this work respectively
have been asserted by them in accordance with the
Copyrights, Designs and Patents Act 1988.

ISBN 978 1 4081 0436 1

A CIP catalogue for this book is available from the British Library.

This book is produced using paper that is made from wood grown
in managed, sustainable forests. It is natural, renewable and
recyclable. The logging and manufacturing processes conform
to the environmental regulations of the country of origin.

Printed and bound in Great Britain
by CPI Cox & Wyman, Reading, RG1 8EX.

Contents

List of characters

Theseus, *the Big Boss*
Hippolyta, *engaged to Theseus*
Philostrate, *Master of the Revels*
Egeus, *father to Hermia*
Hermia, *daughter of Egeus, in love with Lysander*
Demetrius, *in love with Hermia*
Lysander, *in love with Hermia*
Helena, *in love with Demetrius*
Quince, *drama student*
Bottom, *drama student*
Flute, *drama student*
Starveling, *drama student*
Snug, *drama student*
Oberon, *king of the fairies*
Titania, *queen of the fairies*
Puck *or* Robin Goodfellow, *elf*
Peaseblossom, *fairy*
Cobweb, *fairy*
Moth, *fairy*
Mustardseed, *fairy*

Act One

You could tell by his house that Theseus was not without a bob or two. Big, it was. Detached. Garden like a public park.

Some people reckoned Hippolyta was marrying him for his brass. Once, she'd been active in the women's movement. A bra-burning Amazon. Now, suddenly, here she was, engaged to the neighbourhood tycoon. It just didn't sound like her.

Nobody commented openly about any of this. Theseus was a dangerous guy; you didn't poke your nose into his business unless you wanted it chewed off. Plus Hippolyta had taken a few assertiveness courses in her time. Let *her* catch you rabbiting on and you'd end up sweeping your teeth off the floor. They were getting married, Theseus was happy about it and that was that.

In fact, Theseus could hardly wait. Now they stood side by side, in the big bay window, gazing down the garden. His arm was round her waist. He gave her a squeeze, and sighed. 'Not long now, sweetheart. Four days. Dragging a bit, though.'

Hippolyta laughed. 'Don't be such a wimp, Theseus, you big girl's blouse.' Hippolyta was probably the only person in the world who could call Theseus a big girl's blouse without waking up in hospital. 'It'll pass in no time. Know why?'

Theseus shook his head. 'You tell me, sweetie pie.'

'Well, for a start, we'll spend nearly half the time sleeping. You don't know time's passing when you're asleep.' She dug him in the ribs. 'We'll dream. You can be in my dream if I can be in yours.'

Theseus squeezed her waist again, and turned to Philostrate, who'd been admiring a picture on the wall. Philostrate was the guy that Theseus had hired to arrange the wedding reception, organise the marquee, see to it that there'd be enough chairs, supervise the caterers, line up a photographer, find an

10

act of some sort to entertain the guests, and generally make sure the whole thing went off without a glitch.

'Phil? Why don't you go check the post? See who else has RSVP'd. Let's hope we get more fun people than sentimental ones. Can't be doing with folk having a good cry all over the place when I haven't even tortured 'em.'

Philostrate scribbled a memo in his notebook and left. He was a professional. Everything would be fine.

Theseus turned fondly to Hippolyta. 'Have I ever told you, Hippo, how much...'

'Don't call me Hippo,' snarled Hippolyta. 'Makes me sound obese. If you *must* abbreviate my name, what's wrong with Lyta?'

'Lyta, then,' smiled Theseus. 'Have I ever...'

Somebody knocked on the door. Theseus sighed and called, 'Come in.'

The door opened to reveal Egeus, a manager in one of the tycoon's enterprises. He had his daughter with him, and two young men Theseus hardly knew. Egeus looked nervous.

'I ... er, hope we haven't interrupted something important, sir. I know how busy you must be at this time.'

Theseus shook his head. 'Don't worry about it. What can we do for you, Egeus?'

The manager indicated the girl beside him. 'It's my daughter, Hermia. I've arranged a marriage for her, to this young man.' He nodded toward one of the youths. 'His name's Demetrius. He's a good lad. Steady. Make a very suitable husband. But she says no, won't have him at any price. I've tried every way I know to persuade her. She won't budge.'

Theseus gazed at the girl. 'You must obey your father, child. It's the way I like things done, and you know what tends to happen to people who upset me, don't you?'

Hermia held the tycoon's gaze. 'I do, sir, but I love this man.' She pointed. 'His name's Lysander, and I'll marry only him.'

'*Lysander*,' spat Egeus. 'Worthless youth. All *he* has to offer is his pretty face and some flattering words. You can't feed a family on poncy hairdos and poems.' He appealed to Theseus. 'If my daughter persists in her refusal to marry Demetrius, I fear I'll have no option but to do her in, or banish her from society. I hope you'll back me up, sir.'

Theseus looked at Hermia. 'Do you understand your situation, girl? Defy your father, defy *me*, and you'll either die or be sent far away to live the life of a drudge. Such is the fate of a disobedient daughter.'

Hermia shook her head. 'Lysander is as good as Demetrius, sir.'

Theseus nodded. 'I dare say he is, but your father approves of Demetrius, not Lysander.'

'Well then, let my *father* marry Demetrius and I'll marry Lysander.'

Theseus frowned. 'You have until May Day to reflect, Hermia. That's four days. On that day, Hippolyta and I will marry, and if you haven't consented by then to marry Demetrius, you'll suffer the consequences.' He turned to Egeus. 'Come with me, Egeus. You, too, Demetrius. I need to speak to you in private.'

The three men left, followed by Hippolyta. As soon as they were alone, Lysander turned to his love. 'Listen, Hermia,' he murmured, 'we don't have long. I've got an auntie who lives miles away from here. We can go to her, she'll put us up, hide us. We can marry there, and there'll be nothing anybody can do about it.'

Hermia nodded. 'What d'you want me to do?'

Lysander gripped her shoulders and looked into her eyes. 'Remember the wood – Cottingley Wood – where I saw you once with Helena?'

'Yes.'

'Meet me there tomorrow night. *Will* you?'

The girl's eyes shone. 'Try and stop me!'

'Good.' Lysander glanced towards the door. 'Sssh! Here comes Helena now.'

Hermia composed herself, and smiled as her friend walked in. 'Hi, gorgeous, where you off to?'

'Gorgeous, *me*?' Helena scoffed. 'I wish I *was* gorgeous: drop-dead gorgeous, then Demetrius might love me instead of you.'

Hermia shrugged. 'I don't know what he sees in me, Helena, I really don't. I try to shake him off, but the more I diss him, the harder he chases me. The more I hate him, the more he loves me. 'Tisn't *my* fault he's daft.' She smiled and whispered, 'Never mind, listen. Demetrius won't be seeing me any more. We're off tomorrow night, Helena. Me and Lysander. We'll meet in Cottingley Wood, where you and I used to play. Then it's away, where nobody will ever find us.'

15

Helena looked at Lysander, who nodded.

Hermia touched her friend's arm. 'Wish us luck, Helena. I hope things work out for you with Demetrius.'

When the two conspirators had left, Helena sat thinking. *If I warn Demetrius that Hermia's eloping, she thought, perhaps he'll be grateful to me. That's not much, but it's better than being ignored. And who knows: when he sees how determined Hermia is to dump him, maybe he'll turn to me for consolation. How cool will that be?*

☙❧

With six guys in it, Quince's bedsit was packed. Quince sat on the bed and looked at the five lads sitting crosslegged on his floor. They were all on the dole, doing a drama course at college to pass the time.

'All here, are we?'

'You could call the register, like at college,' suggested Bottom sarcastically.

Everybody groaned. College is an OK

place to hang out when you're unemployed, but they do tend to treat you like kids.

Quince ignored the sarcasm. 'I've got all your names in this notebook. I'll sing 'em out, and you can say "Present, sir".'

Bottom shook his head. 'Why don't you tell us about this gig you've landed us – this play we're supposed to do at Theseus's wedding reception? Like, what's it *called*, what's it *about*, stuff like that? We need to know.'

Quince nodded. 'It's called *The Most Lamentable Comedy and Most Cruel Death of Pyramus and Thisby.*'

'Terrific,' said Bottom. 'I do love a nice snappy title, don't you?' Titters from the others. He looked at Quince. 'So what's the *dramatis personae*, and who's playing whom?'

'*Dramatis personae*?' sneered Quince. '*Whom*? What are you doing, Bottom – practising for mingling with Theseus's posh guests at the reception?'

'Am I hummer,' denied Bottom. 'There's nowt wrong with talking the Queen's English. Just tell us our parts.'

Quince consulted his notebook. 'You're playing Pyramus.'

Bottom nodded. 'OK, and what *is* he – a soldier, a dictator or what?'

'He's a lover. Dies heroically for love.'

'Ah, so it's a tearjerker! Well, I hope these wedding guests bring plenty of Kleenex, 'cause I've been known to make *stones* weep. Mind you, I'm cut out more for your ultra-violent roles, really.'

Quince ignored this, too. 'Flute,' he said, 'you'll do Thisby.'

'And what's he – a knight errant?' asked Flute.

'He's a *she*,' Quince told him. 'The woman Pyramus loves.'

Flute shook his head. 'I can't play a woman – I've just started growing a beard.'

'Doesn't matter,' said Quince, 'you'll be

wearing a mask, and you're good at the pale pink voice – we've heard you.'

'I could play Thisby *and* Pyramus,' offered Bottom, 'since I'd be masked. *I* do a good woman's voice.'

'No,' ruled Quince. 'You're Pyramus, Flute's Thisby – it's settled.'

'Get on with it then,' growled Bottom.

'Starveling?'

'Present, sir,' said Starveling.

'You're Thisby's mother. Snout?'

'What?' mumbled Snout.

'You'll play Pyramus's father. I'll do Thisby's father myself. Snug – you're the lion.' Quince closed his notebook and smiled. 'All done. Any questions?'

Snug raised a hand. 'Have you got a copy of the lion's part I could borrow? I'm a bit slow learning lines.'

Quince shook his head. 'You have no lines, Snug. It's just roaring.'

'Let *me* play the lion,' cried Bottom. '*I'll*

19

show you roaring. I'll roar so loud, Theseus'll know he's not the only big noise round here.'

'Yeah, right,' growled Quince. 'But you'll scare his bride spitless, and he'll send some of his lads round to rearrange our bones.'

Bottom shook his head. 'I don't *have* to roar loud, Quince. I could roar like a dove, or even a nightingale.'

Quince sighed. 'Knock it off, Bottom, for Pete's sake. You're playing Pyramus, a gentleman. It's the perfect part for you.'

'What sort of beard should I wear?'

Quince shrugged. 'Makes no odds. Any sort. You could be cleanshaven, if you like.' He turned to the others. 'Listen. Take your parts and learn them by tomorrow night. We'll meet in the wood, where we won't be disturbed, and rehearse. We don't want anybody knowing before the wedding what we're going to do. Now, I'm off to make a list of props we'll steal or borrow. Meanwhile, learn your lines off pat, before we meet tomorrow.'

Act Two

Cottingley Wood was known to harbour fairies, and it was the place that the fairy queen, Titania, had chosen to stay while waiting to bless Theseus and Hippolyta on their wedding night. The wood was close to Theseus's house, which made it handy.

Oberon had chosen it for the same reason. He was king of the fairies, and wanted to bless the happy couple, too. Trouble was, he and Titania were in the middle of a terrific row over an Indian boy that she had and he coveted. Cottingley Wood wasn't very big, and the two were almost certain to bump into each other while staying there. To make matters worse, Oberon had brought along his attendant, Puck, a mischievous elf who was also known as Robin Goodfellow.

On the evening Hermia and Lysander were due to meet in the wood, Puck encountered a fairy there.

'Hi,' grinned the elf. 'Where've *you* blown in from?'

'Everywhere,' answered the fairy. 'I serve our queen, Titania. It means a lot of travelling.' She glanced about her. 'In fact, I'd better be getting on – she's due here any minute with her retinue.'

Puck pulled a face. 'That's awkward. King Oberon'll be here shortly with *his*. You'd better warn your mistress: he's still mad at her.'

The fairy looked at the elf. 'You're Robin Goodfellow, aren't you? The one who plays practical jokes all the time? You serve King Oberon, who likes that sort of thing.'

Puck nodded. 'Correct – not much gets by *you*. And *whoops*, speak of the devil, here's Oberon now.'

'And there's Titania!' cried the fairy. 'How they'll row. I hate that kind of stuff – I'm outta here.'

As the fairy flew off, Titania and Oberon practically bumped into each other.

'Ill met by moonlight, proud Titania,' growled Oberon.

Titania smiled. 'Still jealous are we, Oberon?' She looked at him. 'You're here for the wedding, I suppose. Theseus and Hippolyta? You mean to bring them luck, but the world's gone mad since you and I fell out. We've had spring in winter, frost in June, floods the year round, till we can't tell the seasons apart.'

'Then stop defying me,' snapped Oberon. 'All you have to do is give me that boy, and everything'll get back to normal.'

Titania shook her head. 'His mother was my friend. She died giving birth to him. That's why I'm looking after him. I can never give him up.'

'Huh!' Oberon glowered. 'And how long do you plan to stay in this wood?'

'Till after the wedding.' Titania smiled. 'We intend to celebrate the occasion, join us if you wish!'

'Give me the boy and I might.'

'Not for all your kingdom.' Titania turned

to her retinue. 'Come, fairies, let us leave. There'll be bloodshed if we stay here longer.'

'Go then!' cried Oberon, as Titania departed. 'I'll get even before you leave Cottingley, see if I don't.' He called to his elf. 'Puck?'

'I'm here.'

'Did I ever tell you about the time I saw Cupid loose one of his arrows at somebody, and he missed, and the arrow fell on a certain white flower? The flower turned purple, and girls call it *Love in Idleness*?'

'You told me.'

'Well, I want you to bring me the juice of that flower.' He smiled. 'If a drop of the juice gets onto someone's eyelid while they sleep, they'll fall in love with the first creature they see on waking. I want you to fly as fast as you can to where that flower grows.'

Puck nodded. 'I'll put a girdle round about the earth in forty minutes,' he boasted.

With Puck in orbit, Oberon felt quite smug.

I'll make Titania fall in love with something really bizarre, he promised himself, *and I won't let her have the antidote till she gives me the Indian boy.*

He heard a sound. 'Somebody's coming – two mortals. I'm invisible to them, I'll stay and earwig.'

The two mortals were Demetrius and Helena.

As Oberon watched and listened, Demetrius turned on the miserable girl and snarled, 'I don't love you at all, Helena. In fact it makes me puke to look at you, so I don't know why you bother following me.' He peered all around. 'Where *are* Lysander and Hermia? You said they'd be here. I'm going to kill *him* and drag *her* back to her father.'

'I can't *help* following you,' wailed Helena. 'I'm under your spell.'

Demetrius scoffed. 'Do I speak tenderly to you? Lead you on? No, I don't, so leave. It's dangerous in the wood at night, and

I'm not going to protect you.'

'If I could *fight* for your love, I would,' cried Helena. 'But girls can't. We're made to be wooed, not to woo.'

'Get *lost*, will you?' Demetrius spun on his heel and plunged into the shadow under the trees.

Helena stumbled after him as best she could.

Oberon followed the pathetic girl with his eyes. 'I'll promise you this, sweetheart,' he murmured. 'Before that lad leaves the wood, it'll be him following you, and you won't want to know.'

As the two mortals moved away, Puck appeared.

Oberon looked at him. 'Did you find the flower?'

'I did.'

'Let me have it.'

The elf handed over a handful of purple blooms.

Oberon grinned. 'I know a bank where the wild thyme blows,' he murmured. 'Titania often sleeps there. I'll find her, paint her eyelids with the juice from these.' He divided the bunch, gave half back to Puck. 'Take these, and go after the mortals who were here. The lady loves the youth, but he disdains her. Paint his eyes, and make sure the lady's the first thing he'll see when he wakes. Meet me here at dawn.'

❧

As Puck and Oberon were parting, in another part of the wood, Titania was preparing to sleep.

'Come, fairies,' she commanded, 'and sing me to sleep with a lullaby.' She lay with her head on a cushion of thyme, and closed her eyes.

The fairies sang so sweetly that their queen was soon asleep. Leaving one of their number to watch over her, they dispersed to carry out the various tasks she had set for them. Some were to cure buds that might otherwise rot. Others must hunt down tiny bats, and take their leathery wings to be turned into coats for Titania's elves. And some were commanded to drive away owls whose hooting might disturb their mistress's sleep.

The fairies had not been long gone when Oberon came creeping through the trees. He moved so stealthily that the sentry didn't see him. He bent over the sleeping Titania and squeezed juice from the flowers onto her eyelids.

'What thou seest when thou dost wake,' he whispered, 'do it for thy true love take.' He stood for a moment, gazing down at her, then left as silently as he'd come.

A short time later, Lysander and Hermia reached that part of the wood. 'I think we're a bit lost,' admitted Lysander. 'Maybe we should get some sleep, eh? Wait for daylight.'

'Fine,' murmured Hermia. 'Find yourself a spot to lie on – this bank will do for me.'

'We can *both* lie on the bank,' suggested Lysander. 'Two heads, one pillow.'

'Uh-uh.' Hermia shook her head. 'I'm afraid that's *not* a good idea, my love. I need my space.'

So the lovers found their separate beds, said goodnight and were sound asleep when Puck came wandering in their direction, muttering to himself.

'I see no mortals. No ardent maid, no scornful youth. Wild goose chase if you ask ... hey!' He spotted the lovers. '*That's* them — must be. See how they lie apart when they might lie entwined.' He approached Lysander. 'Misery guts,' he hissed. 'Ignorant wuss. I'll sort *you*, pal, no danger.' He squeezed juice onto the lad's eyelids, cackled to himself, and caught a lift with a breeze that was going his way.

No sooner had Puck left, than Demetrius appeared, running, with Helena stumbling after him.

31

'Stop!' gasped the desperate girl. 'I can't run any more.'

'Get away from me,' snarled Demetrius. 'Go home.'

'You won't leave me here in the dark, my love?'

'You better believe it, Helena. I'm off.' Demetrius ran on, leaving the girl bent over, fighting for breath.

'I wish,' she gasped, 'that I looked like Hermia – had her sparkling eyes. He wouldn't run from me *then*. In fact he'd probably...' She broke off. A short distance away, somebody was lying on the ground. Helena approached cautiously, holding her breath.

'Lysander!' She spoke his name aloud, mightily relieved that she was no longer alone. The thought crossed her mind that he might be dead, but then he woke and saw her.

'Oh, Helena!' he groaned, scrambling to his feet. 'Have I told you how deeply I love you – that I'd run through fire for you?' He glanced wildly all around. 'Where's that Demetrius? I'll *kill* him.'

'Why?' cried Helena. 'Just because he loves Hermia? Hermia loves only *you* – can't you be satisfied with that?'

'Satisfied?' scoffed Lysander. 'With *Hermia*? Are you having a laugh? I told you, Helena – it's *you* I adore.'

Helena shook her head. 'No, it's *not*, Lysander. You ran away with Hermia – defied her father and Theseus. You're risking death for her sake, so why mock me? It's bad enough that Demetrius won't look at me, without *you* laughing at me as well.' She backed off. 'I thought you were more of a gentleman than this, Lysander. I hoped you'd look after me till daylight, but I won't stay to be made a fool of.' She hurried away, weeping.

Lysander gazed after Helena, then glanced across to where Hermia lay, still sleeping.

'She didn't notice you, Hermia, and from this moment on, neither will I. I'll follow Helena, the light of my life, and serve her in every way I can.'

As Lysander dashed away into the dark, Hermia woke with a cry. 'Aaagh! Get this snake off me – get it off!' She sat up, and the nightmare began to dissolve. She looked over to where Lysander had been sleeping. There was only a patch of flattened grass. 'Lysander?' She glanced around, called again. 'Lysander – can you hear me?' She set off through the trees. She called and called, receiving no reply. 'I'll find him,' vowed the maid, 'or else I'll die.'

Act Three

On her comfortable bank, Titania continued to sleep. She was unaware that six mortals had gathered nearby, intent on rehearsing the play they were going to put on at the wedding of Theseus and Hippolyta. None of them saw the fairy queen, who was visible to mortals only when she chose to be.

'All here, are we?' asked Bottom.

'We are,' Quince told him, 'and what a cool spot to rehearse. Look – short grass for a stage, and that hawthorn bush for the wings.' He looked at his fellow students. 'We won't read through – we'll act out the whole thing, just as it'll be on the night.'

'Quince?' Bottom had his hand up.

'What?'

'I can see problems with this particular play, Quince. A lot of people have issues around the use of weapons, right? And I kill myself with a sword. That could offend.'

'Yes,' agreed Starveling. 'I say we leave that bit out.'

Bottom shook his head. 'No. What we do is, we have a prologue. Something like this: *It's necessary to the story that Pyramus kill himself with a sword. However, both producer and cast wish to make it clear that they deeply deplore the use of weapons against human beings in all circumstances. The swordplay you will witness is for dramatic effect only, and on no account should anybody interpret it as a glorification of terrorism: nor should anybody try it at home.*'

Quince nodded. 'That ought to do it.' He frowned. 'What's up *now*, Snout?'

'The lion, Quince. Protected species, you know, lions. They only attack humans if they're cornered, and here we are slandering 'em by pretending they constitute a threat. Won't play well with the conservation lobby, I can tell you that.'

'Another prologue,' suggested Bottom, 'to be spoken by Snug himself. It could go like this: *For the purpose of the play, we intend to portray the lion as a fearsome beast. In reality, each one of us is acutely aware of the plight of lions in the wild, and a percentage of the proceeds of tonight's performance will be donated to the World Wildlife Fund. In addition, we wish to assure our patrons that no animal will be harmed in the staging of this play.'*

Quince nodded. 'OK, we'll include both prologues, but there are a couple of other snags. One is finding a way to represent moonlight when we'll be doing the thing indoors. This is vital, because the story says Pyramus and Thisby meet by moonlight. The other is there needs to be a wall. Obviously we can't drag a wall into Theseus's mansion if we want to keep our kneecaps, so somebody will have to *be* Wall.' He sighed. 'One of us will probably have to be Moonshine as well, so we'd better get it sorted. Snout, you can double as Pyramus's father and Wall. Starveling will have to do Thisby's mother and Moonshine. All right, Pyramus, it's you to begin.'

As Bottom opened his mouth to speak, Puck arrived on the scene.

'Hey up!' exclaimed the elf. 'Who're *these* wurzels, so close to Titania's bed?' He was invisible to mortals, so he stayed to eavesdrop. 'Ah!' he breathed as Bottom delivered the opening line. 'It's a *play*. I'll be the audience.' He grinned. 'I might even *do* something, if I get the chance.'

His chance wasn't long in coming. Bottom had to exit stage and then re-enter. While the actor waited behind the hawthorn bush, Puck cast a spell, which gave him the head of an ass. There was no mirror, so Bottom couldn't see his ghastly transformation. He re-entered, ready to continue.

Quince took one look and screamed, 'Look out – aliens have taken him over. Run! Run for your lives!' The students fled into the trees, leaving poor Bottom with Puck. He couldn't see the elf, so thought he was alone. 'What's up with them?' he cried aloud. 'It's a trick –

40

they're trying to make me scared.'

Snout came back. He stared at his friend, aghast. 'I d-d-don't understand, Bottom,' he stammered. 'Who's done this to you?'

He ran off again and Quince reappeared.

'Lord help you, Bottom, you haven't half changed.' Then he too fled.

Bottom yelled after them. '*I* know what you're up to. You're trying to make an ass of me, aren't you? Well, it isn't going to work.' *I'll stay here*, he told himself. *I'll stroll around and sing. I'll show 'em they can't scare me.*

He started to sing:

'Love, love changes everything,

Da da daa-da, daa daa dee...'

At the sound of his voice, Titania woke with a start. 'What – what angel wakes me from my flowery bed?' she cried.

Bottom, who couldn't see her, sang on:

'Doo, doo doo doo dum-di-dum,

Doo di dah dah, doo di dung...'

Enraptured, the fairy queen begged the

41

singer not to stop. 'Sing it again,' she moaned. '*Again.* Your voice is as beautiful as your face, as your *body*.' She made herself visible to the ass-headed monster, who seemed perfect to her because of the juice on her eyelids. 'I love you,' she sighed. 'Oh, how I love you.'

Bottom goggled at the gorgeous fairy. He couldn't believe his luck – thought he must be dreaming. *She's one hundred per cent fit, this one*, he told himself. *I'm well in here and no mistake*. The lovely creature was offering him servants, jewels, soft beds to lie on, if he'd only consent to stay with her for ever.

As he stood, spellbound, the smitten Titania summoned her attendants. 'Peaseblossom! Cobweb! Moth! Mustardseed!'

They appeared at once, and their queen commanded them to lavish on her beloved every possible care. The fairies saw only a mortal with the head of an ass, but Titania was their queen, to be obeyed at once without question.

Bottom sighed with contentment: he'd never felt so chuffed.

❧

In another part of the wood, Oberon paced, impatient for Puck to report back. *I wonder if Titania's awake yet?* he fretted, *and if so, what sort of creature is she mooning over?*

He hadn't long to wonder. Puck blew in, looking as pleased as Punch.

'Now then, madcap,' greeted Oberon. 'How did it go?'

Puck told him about the students, their rehearsal, and the trick he'd played on Bottom. 'His mates all freaked when they saw his makeover,' he laughed. 'I wish you'd been there – it was classic. And that wasn't the best bit. The best bit was when the donkey-headed plonker woke Titania with his braying, and she fell bonce over bum in love with him.'

Oberon slapped his knees. 'Even better

than I expected,' he laughed. 'And the other mortal – the disdainful lover – you managed to anoint his eyelids with the juice?'

Puck nodded. 'I did. The scorned maid lay close by – he's sure to see her first when he wakes up.'

'Splendid.' Oberon rubbed his hands together. 'A fine night's work, little friend, though I say it myself.'

The pair were still congratulating themselves when Demetrius appeared with Hermia.

'Sssh,' hissed Oberon, 'here's the man himself!'

Puck shook his head. 'That's the maid all right, but it's a different guy.'

The two mortals were yelling at each other. 'Why don't you get off my case?' cried Demetrius. 'I *love* you. Save your anger for your enemy.'

'You *are* my enemy,' screeched Hermia. 'You killed my precious Lysander.'

The youth shook his head. 'No, I did not. I haven't even *seen* him.'

'Yes, you have, Demetrius. You *must* have. He wouldn't have walked away in the night and left me sleeping.'

The youth shrugged. 'I haven't seen him, I tell you. He's alive as far as I know.'

'Ha!' spat Hermia. 'It's a waste of time talking to you. I'm off, and if I never set eyes on you again it'll be too soon.'

She strode away. Demetrius watched her go and shook his head. It was useless trying to reason with her in that mood, and anyway he was shattered. He decided to grab a nap, and lay down.

Oberon looked at the elf. 'Looks like you fouled up big time, Puck. Juiced the wrong guy. Listen, go find the maid, Helena, quick as you like. Bring her here. Tell her lies if you have to, just get her here. Meanwhile, I'll juice this lad's eyes, so she'll be the first thing they light on when he wakes.'

45

'Watch,' grinned the elf. 'Now you see me – now you don't.'

Oberon bent over the sleeping youth and spoke a spell, dribbling juice onto his eyelids.

Presently Puck returned. 'I found Helena,' he chirped. 'She'll be here in a minute. The guy I juiced by mistake is with her, trying to get her interested.' He grinned. 'Can we stay and watch? Lord, what fools these mortals be!'

'Sssh!' Oberon pulled the elf aside. 'Their noise will wake Demetrius.'

'I know, and he'll fall for Helena, then she'll have *both* guys after her.' Puck rubbed his hands together. 'Don't you just love a really impossible situation?'

Helena appeared looking harrassed, with Lysander at her heels. The youth was pawing her arm, pleading. 'Why won't you believe me when I say I love you? Look – I'm *crying*, for Pete's sake.'

Helena scoffed. 'You're mocking me. You love Hermia, not me.'

'I *thought* I loved Hermia,' protested Lysander. 'I asked her to elope with me, but I wasn't thinking straight. She's nothing compared to you.'

As Puck had hoped, their quarreling woke Demetrius. His eyes fell on Helena.

'Phooarrh!' he growled. 'Where've you been all my life, sweetheart? Come here, let me...'

'Oh yeah,' sneered Helena. '*I* get it. The two of you are in it together, aren't you? *Let's make fun of the ugly one.* If you were *real* men, you wouldn't treat a girl like this.'

The bewitched youths eyed each other.

'Why are you doing this, Demetrius?' demanded Lysander. 'You love Hermia.' He spread his hands. 'She and I were eloping, but I've gone off the idea, right? I *give* her to you, and claim Helena for myself.'

'You're *both* wasting your breath,' grated Helena.

'Stick to your plan, Lysander,' spat

Demetrius. 'Run away with Hermia. 'See – here she comes now. *She's* the one for you.'

Hermia approached, distressed. She looked at Lysander. 'I could hear your voice a mile off,' she said. 'But what about our plan? Why did you leave me by myself in the wood?'

'I had to follow Helena, didn't I?' said Lysander.

'*Why*?' asked Hermia. 'You said you loved *me*. We were eloping, running off to get married. I didn't think *anything* could change your mind about that.'

Lysander scoffed. 'I *hate* you, Hermia. Hate you and love Helena. *That's* why I left.'

Hermia shook her head. 'You're lying, you *must* be.'

Helena's bewildered gaze went from Hermia to Lysander to Demetrius. 'It's all *three* of you, isn't it?' she cried. 'You've all got together to make a prat out of me.' She looked at Hermia. 'We were mates at school,'

48

she choked. 'How can *you*, of all people, turn on me like this?'

Hermia shook her head. 'I don't know what you're talking about, Helena,' she protested. '*I* don't want to make a prat out of you – *you* seem to be making a prat out of *me*.'

'I don't believe you!' cried Helena. 'I can *see* you, you know, the three of you – pulling faces behind my back, winking at one another. Well, I won't stay to be treated like this – I'm off.'

'Please, Helena,' pleaded Lysander. 'Don't go – listen to what I'm saying. I love you more than anything in the world.'

'Yeah, right!' sneered Helena.

'Don't listen to him,' said Demetrius. 'It's me – *I'm* the one who loves you.'

'Oh!' gasped Helena. 'You're all being unbelievably cruel. And *you*,' she turned on Hermia. 'You're worse than the men, you … midget.'

'*Midget*?' Hermia looked at her former

friend. 'That's *so* heightist. I bet you've been comparing your tallness to mine, haven't you, you pathetic stick of spaghetti? *That's* how you've turned them against me. Well...' She started towards Helena. 'I may be short, but I can reach high enough to scratch your eyes out!'

Helena backed off. 'I'll go, since you all seem determined to continue mocking me with declarations of undying love, which can't possibly be true for one as *plain* as me.'

'Yes, *go!*' snarled Hermia.

⌒⌒⌒

Puck and Oberon watched as the mortals left: the maids separately, the youths together. 'Looks like you messed up again,' said Oberon. 'Either that, or you do these things on purpose to amuse yourself.'

Puck shook his head. 'It was a mistake, Oberon. The mortal youths look much the same. I juiced the wrong one, that's all. Mind you...' he grinned. 'I'm not sorry.

I like nothing better than screwing up the affairs of mortals.'

'Yes, well.' Oberon looked severe. 'I think those two youths have gone off to fight over Helena, and it's not funny. Somebody could get hurt or even killed. Listen, I want you to create a fog. A really dense one, so thick they can't see each other at all. And then I want you to go about, calling out to Demetrius in Lysander's voice, and to Lysander in Demetrius's voice.' He smiled. 'That way, they'll strike and strike without harming each other. And when they've tired themselves out slashing fog and have gone to sleep, put some of this juice in Lysander's eyes. It's the antidote to the love juice. When he wakes, he won't want Helena any more – he'll be in love with Hermia again, which is how it ought to be. Meanwhile I'll find Titania, make her swap the Indian boy for the antidote, so she'll be free of that ass-headed monstrosity. Though she's under my spell, I think a part of her knows she's being made a fool of, and I find myself feeling sorry for her. So ... two drops of juice, two pairs of sleeping eyes, and all will be well 'ere the morning sun doth rise.'

Act Four

Puck's fog was a serious peasouper. Lysander stood with clenched fists, peering into the opaque vapour.

'Demetrius, you creepazoid, where *are* you?'

'Right here,' mimicked Puck. 'You blind idiot.'

'Good – stand still while I rip your head off. Hunnnh! – *missed.*'

'Yes, 'cause you're a blind idiot.'

Some distance off stood the *real* Demetrius, turning on the spot, lashing out in all directions. 'Stand *still*, Lysander, you snivelling coward. I'm only going to ram my fingers up your nose and pull an eyeball down.'

'Sorry,' said Puck as Lysander. 'Don't fancy it.'

'Think *I* care what you fancy?' roared Demetrius. He lunged at the voice, landing a solid punch on a tree trunk. '*Oooowww – my flippin' knuckles!*' He danced in agony, flapping his ruined hand.

Meanwhile, Lysander had burned himself out chasing phantoms. He stood still and yawned. 'Night *and* fog,' he growled. 'Deadly combination. I'll get some rest, track down that wuss Demetrius in the morning.' He lay down. Nearby, his rival was doing the same, and in another part of the wood slept Helena and Hermia, each unaware of the other's proximity.

༄

As the four exhausted mortals lay sleeping, a group approached that included the lovers Titania and Bottom, the attendants Peaseblossom, Cobweb, Moth, Mustardseed and other fairies. Some of these fairies had once been photographed here in Cottingley Wood by two young mortal girls. The snapshots had appeared in books and magazines all over the world, and the fairies were finding it difficult to get over themselves because of it. Behind this group, undetected, came Oberon.

Titania smiled fondly at Bottom. 'Sit down on this flowery bed, my love. I want to caress your cheek, twist flowers into your hair and kiss those gorgeous big ears.'

The couple reclined on the grass, and Titania proceded to do those things. Bottom smiled contentedly, as well he might, and looked around.

'Where's Peasblossom?' he demanded.

'I'm here,' said that fairy.

'Scratch my head, will you, Peaseblossom? Where's Cobweb?'

'Ready,' said Cobweb.

'Ah, Cobweb.' Bottom treated the attendant to his ass's smile. 'I want you to find a bumblebee and nick its honey-bag. Take it easy mind – there's no rush. Bring me the honey, and be careful not to slosh it around. Don't want you pickling yourself. Mustardseed?'

'Here,' answered Mustardseed. 'How may I help you?'

'The scratching,' yawned Bottom. 'Just help with the scratching, will you? My face feels hairy, can't think why.'

'Perhaps my handsome darling would like to hear some music?' suggested Titania.

'Oh, aye!' nodded Bottom. 'Partial to a bit of music, I am. Let's have somebody play the tongs, and somebody else the bones.'

'And what about food? What will you eat, my prince?'

'I could murder a helping of dry oats,' requested Bottom, 'washed down with a bottle of hay. Can't beat a good bottle of hay when you've a thirst on, I always say.'

Titania pulled a face. 'Sounds absolutely ghastly, my dear, but there's a brave fairy standing by who'll track down a squirrel's hoard and bring you fresh nuts.'

Bottom shook his monstrous head. 'I'd sooner have a handful or two of dried peas, but never mind. I feel fatigued suddenly. Tell your fairies not to bother me with anything –

I fancy a nap.'

'Of course, my love,' crooned Titania. 'Let me hold you in my arms while you sleep.' She turned to her retinue. 'Make yourselves scarce,' she commanded. 'Go on – scram.' She twined herself round Bottom. 'I'm crazy about you, you handsome hunk,' she murmured. 'Crazy.'

❧

Oberon, who'd watched all this, looked round as Puck appeared. He indicated the ill-matched couple on the ground. 'Look at the state of this, Puck. I was watching her a few minutes ago, fawning on this donkey-headed numpty. She was weaving flowers into his hair, if you can believe it. And when I mocked her for it, she asked me to bear with her. Asked me softly, y'know? Which can only be because she realises deep down she's being a plonker. And since she seemed to be feeling soft, I took the opportunity to ask her for the Indian boy.' Oberon shrugged, pulled a face.

'And she gave him to me, just like that. I couldn't believe it. He's in my bower right now, in fairyland. So now...' Oberon showed Puck the antidote. 'I'm going to take the spell off.' He pointed to Bottom. 'And then you'd better get rid of that ass's head, so this rude mechanical can wake like the others and get himself home.' He smiled. 'They won't remember anything that's happened to them while they were bewitched, except in the form of those vague memories you get when you wake after dreaming.'

Oberon administered the antidote, and Titania woke up.

'Oh, it's *you*, Oberon,' she mumbled. 'D'you know, I dreamed I was madly in love with an *ass*!'

Oberon smiled. 'And so you *were*, my dear – there he lies.'

'Ugh!' Titania jerked herself clear of the sleeping Bottom. 'How the devil could such a thing *happen*? He's totally hideous!'

Oberon laughed. 'Don't worry about it, Titania – stuff happens, that's all. Let's have some music – perhaps it will wake these mortals who've taken to dossing in the wood.'

'Aye, let them wake,' cried Puck, 'and see things through their *own* eyes!'

'Let them rest,' chuckled Oberon. 'Tonight we dance and sing in celebration of the coming festivities, and tomorrow we'll go to Theseus's house, where we'll bless his union with Hippolyta, and see these lately bewildered couples wed, so that all ends happily.'

᪣᪤

Early next morning, their wedding ceremony behind them, Theseus and Hippolyta decided to spend the day in the countryside. Strolling through Cottingley Wood in the company of Egeus and a squad of minders, they happened on the place where the four young people lay sleeping.

'Who're these?' exclaimed Theseus.

'It's my daughter, Hermia,' cried Egeus, 'with Lysander, Demetrius and her friend, Helena. What on *earth* are they doing out here?'

'They were probably celebrating May Day,' said Theseus. 'They heard Hippolyta and I planned to come this way, and stayed to congratulate us.' He frowned at Egeus. 'Isn't it today your daughter has to decide whether to obey you and marry Demetrius, or face death or banishment?'

Egeus nodded grimly. 'It is indeed.'

'Then we must wake them and know Hermia's decision.'

The youngsters were quickly wakened. Their hearts kicked them in the ribs when they saw who was gazing down at them. Nobody messes with Theseus. They scrambled to their feet, knocking dust and grass from their clothes with their hands. 'S-s-sorry,' stammered Lysander, 'we were just...'

'What puzzles *me*,' interrupted Theseus, 'is how you and Demetrius can lie down and sleep within a foot of each other, when everybody knows you're bitter rivals.'

Lysander shook his head. 'This is going to sound weird, but I don't really remember how I got here. I was ... Hermia and I were to meet, and we were going to run off where nobody'd ever...'

'See!' cried Egeus. 'He admits it – he was going to rob Demetrius of a wife, and me of a daughter.'

'Yes,' nodded Demetrius. 'Helena warned me of their plan – I came to intercept them, and Helena followed me. And then...' He broke off, shook his head. 'And then suddenly I didn't love Hermia any more – I loved Helena. I know that all sounds crazy and I can't explain. It happened, that's all I can say. And I know I'll love Helena for ever.'

Theseus shook his head. 'Amazing.' He turned to Egeus. 'I'm sorry, old friend, but

I'm going to have to overrule you. This has turned out so conveniently, I'm inclined to believe some higher power has been at work.' He smiled. 'Let's scrap this outing, go back to my place – sorry, dear – *our* place, see these loving couples wed and have a party.'

The four young people watched as Theseus, Hippolyta and Egeus faded among the trees, followed by Theseus's minders. When the group had passed from view, they turned dazed expressions on one another.

'Am I still dreaming,' murmured Demetrius, 'or did Theseus just invite us to a party at his place?'

'It's like a *dream*,' whispered Helena. 'Me and my Demetrius.'

'We *did* dream, I think,' said Lysander. 'I can't really remember.'

'Weddings were mentioned just now,' put in Hermia. 'I certainly didn't dream *that*, so why don't we make our way to Theseus's, and tell each other our dreams as we go?'

Not far away, Bottom was waking from his dream. He couldn't remember what he'd dreamed, except that it was something seriously weird, with a fairy queen in it. The word Peaseblossom drifted across his mind, and something about a hairy face. All nonsense, of course. He was to play Pyramus in a play though – *that* was real enough. What about his friends? Where were Quince, Flute, Snug, Starveling and Snout? They'd been rehearsing with him, hadn't they – here in the wood? Why had they left him alone? He set off home, muttering under his breath:

'The ass I am, I have not *always* been; methinks I embraced a fairy queen.'

Act Five

At Quince's place, the players were panicking. Any minute, Philostrate might send for them. As organiser of tonight's festivities, he'd want to see their play, to satisfy himself that it was fit to be performed in front of Theseus, Hippolyta and their high-powered guests.

Snag was, nobody could find Bottom. 'Have you tried his house?' asked Quince. 'Is he back yet?'

Starveling shook his head. 'They've heard nowt from him – maybe he's gone off with the aliens who remodelled his bonce.'

'That's it then,' groaned Flute. 'We're stuffed. Can't do the play without him, can we?'

Quince shook his head. 'Can we heck. Nobody could step in at such short notice.'

There was a knock at the door. Snug came in.

'Hey, listen – it's not just Theseus and his missus partying tonight. There's two other couples getting wed, and all *their* guests'll be there as well. Just think, if we'd done *Pyramus and Thisby* in front of *that* lot, there'd have been loads of tips, word-of-mouth recommendations, future bookings. We'd have made it, guys – big time.'

'Well, there you go,' said Flute. 'Our big break, and Bottom's blown it.'

'No, he hasn't,' said a familiar voice. Everybody swung round. Bottom stood grinning in the doorway, wearing his own head. 'Weird stuff's gone down with me, lads, I can tell you.'

'Tell us about it,' smiled Quince, who was mightily relieved.

Bottom shook his head. 'Not now. We've got to get our stuff together, and boogie on down to Theseus's place, so we're ready if Philostrate gives us the word.'

❧

At Theseus's house, Hippolyta was puzzling over the stories that Lysander and the other young people had told. 'It's gob-smackingly weird, darling, isn't it?'

'More weird than true, if you ask me,' growled Theseus. 'I can't be doing with all this new age, airy-fairy stuff. It's for poets, vegans and save-the-gay-green-whale types in sandals. Give me the real world any time.'

'What they recall of their experience may *seem* airy-fairy,' argued Hippolyta, 'but it has caused them to commit to one another in a very responsible way.'

Before her husband could respond, the two young couples appeared.

'Speak of the devil,' growled Theseus, 'and here are the newlyweds, full of the joys of spring.' He tried on a smile, turning to them. 'You're all well, I trust?'

'We are indeed,' replied Lysander. 'And we hope the same is true of yourselves.'

'It is,' Theseus told him, 'but we've an important decision to take, which is what show to book that'll pass three hours or so between supper and bedtime?' He glanced around. 'Where's Philostrate?'

'I'm here,' answered the organiser.

'What choices have we, Phil?'

'I've a variety of acts laid on,' said Philostrate. 'Here's the list.' He handed Theseus a paper. 'Just choose whichever you all fancy.'

'Hmmm.' Theseus studied the list. '*Cherry-ripe*, sung by a male soprano to the banjo. Huh! Let him sing to the banjo if he likes – he's not singing to me.'

'There's a play' said Philostrate. 'It's ten words long, which makes it the shortest play *I* ever heard of, and even *then* it's ten words too long. It's tedious, the hero dies, and the company's the most shambolic ever to tread the boards.'

'Who're the players?' asked Theseus.

'Unemployed youths, thick as two short planks, doing a drama course to pass the time.'

Theseus grinned. 'Let's give 'em a chance – why not?'

'No.' The organiser shook his head. 'Their play's not for a sophisticated gentleman like you, Theseus. I've seen it, it's rubbish.' He shrugged. 'Unless of course you feel the sheer unmitigated *badness* of the thing might amuse you.'

Theseus looked at him. 'We'll see it. They're simple people, doing the best they can. That makes it pretty fine, no matter how bad it is. Bring them in.' He turned to his guests. 'Take your seats, everybody.'

Philostrate returned. 'They have a prologue, sir.'

Theseus nodded. 'No problem.'

Quince appeared on stage and recited his prologue. It came across as a bit of a muddle, and the audience was left none the wiser when it was done. Quince bowed and exited. Straight after came a fanfare, and on came Pyramus and Thisby, Wall, Moonshine and

Lion. Quince introduced these characters, then commenced to explain the story of Pyramus and Thisby from start to finish. This done he exited, along with all the characters except Wall.

Snout, playing Wall, then gave his name and told the audience he represented a wall that had a crack in it. 'This crack,' he explained, 'is the very crack that Pyramus and Thisby talk to each other through.'

At this point, Starveling came on, playing Moonshine.

'This man represents Moonshine,' said Wall, 'because Pyramus and Thisby always met by moonlight.'

Lion now entered, and Wall spelled out the beast's part in the story. In the audience, Theseus leaned across and murmured in Demetrius's ear. 'Bet you've never met a wall that spoke better than this one, eh?'

Demetrius chuckled. 'Wittiest partition *I* ever heard, sir.'

These preliminaries being done with, the company commenced to appear according to their cues, and to act out the play. It ran smoothly for the most part, and presently it was time for Lion to perform.

Snug faced the audience and began his prologue. 'For the purpose of the play, we intend to portray the lion as a fearsome beast...'

Theseus whispered again to Demetrius. 'Didn't realise lions could be politically correct.'

'Oh yes,' smiled Demetrius. 'Political correctness has entered the *mane*-stream – geddit?'

'I *cat*-egorically deny that,' quipped Lysander.

Everybody groaned.

'Sssh!' hissed Theseus. 'Listen to the Moonshine.'

Starveling, lantern in hand, intoned, 'This lantern represents the moon, and I'm the Man in the Moon...'

Amused by the ludicrous spectacle before them, the audience was sending everything up.

'If he's the Man in the Moon,' murmured Theseus, 'and the lantern's the moon, why isn't he in the lantern?'

''Cause the candle'd *satellite* to him,' whooped Demetrius.

'You're just trying to *crater* disturbance,' growled Lysander.

'I didn't *planet*,' rejoined Demetrius, seismic with mirth.

On stage, unnoticed, the play reached its tragic end. The audience quelled its laughter as Bottom stepped forward, peering to where Theseus was seated. 'Would you care to hear our epilogue, sir, or watch a dance performed by two of the company?'

Theseus shook his head. 'No epilogue, young man. Your play is a total tragedy, beautifully performed. Let's see the dance.'

As two of the players danced, Theseus turned to his guests. 'It's gone midnight – time to hit the sack.' He smiled. 'I won't be surprised if one or two of us sleep late in the morning.'

The company rose and dispersed, leaving the students to pack up their props.

❧

With the mortals gone, and the house dark and silent, Puck appeared. He carried a broom, with which he commenced to sweep up the party debris.

As the elf worked, Titania and Oberon appeared, their quarrel suspended in the happiness of the occasion. Triple weddings don't happen every day, and the bestowal of so many blessings was going to require all of their energy, leaving none to fuel a grudge.

The fairy attendants flitted from room to room, dancing and singing to bring good fortune to the house, while Oberon and

About the Author

There was no tradition of theatre-going in my working-class family, and I was never exposed to Shakespeare in my youth. Because of this, I have always had difficulty in extracting meaning from the Bard's intricate language while watching a performance. I can sort it out when reading a play: I go *'huh ... what's that he's saying?'* and read the passage again. And, if necessary, again. On stage it's there, then it's gone, and here comes another fancy bit.

I was delighted therefore to be asked to write a simplified prose interpretation of *A Midsummer Night's Dream*, my favourite

Shakespeare play. I feel that if I'd read something like this before seeing the play on stage, I'd have had a clearer idea of what was going on, and been free to revel in the playwright's matchless poetry. I hope this little book will help somebody do just that, and even pass an exam in it!

Meanwhile, I've had fun telling friends I'm having to rewrite Shakespeare because he made such a mess of it. Trouble is, they all know I'm more of an ass than Bottom the weaver, and none of 'em is buying my yarn.

Truth is, I'd trade every line I've ever written, and will ever write, for just one of his.